Enjoy All the S.O.S. Adventures!

By Alan Katz

Illustrated by Alex Lopez

HARPER
An Imprint of HarperCollins*Publishers*

To David, a friendly editor and an editorly friend

—Alan Katz

Library of Congress Control Number: 2021948135

ISBN 978-0-06-300661-4 — ISBN 978-0-06-300660-7 (pbk.)

Typography by Corina Lupp

22 23 24 25 26   PC/LSCC   10 9 8 7 6 5 4 3 2 1

❖

First Edition

TABLE OF CONTENTS

CHAPTER 1

A New Mission

WE'VE MADE IT TO FRIDAY,
AND ALL HAS BEEN FINE.
PLEASE TAKE THIS MESSAGE
AS A SPECIAL BONUS SIGN.

"That's awesome, Mrs. Baltman, really awesome," Milton Worthy said as he entered Room 311B. "I'll bet you stay up all night figuring out these funny rhymes."

"Not really, Milton," his teacher said. "But thank you."

"I mean it, Mrs. B.," Milton continued. "You're like a professional rhymer. Maybe you could open up your own rhyme store."

"A rhyme store? Milton, I don't think there's any such—"

Milton interrupted her before she could say "thing."

"Well, *there should be*!" Milton insisted. "Like . . . people come in with a word, and you give them another word that rhymes with it. You could probably charge ten dollars per rhyme."

"My word! That's absurd!" Mrs. Baltman said.

"See, you're *so* good at it!" Milton responded.

Mrs. Baltman told Milton that she appreciated his kind words, but she doubted that people would pay for rhymes. Then she asked him to take his seat.

Milton got to his desk. He leaned over to share his rhyme store concept with Noah.

"Good morning, Mr. Ferret. Do you want to hear an idea that has merit?"

Milton laughed at his own rhyme. Noah just grumbled. The ferret grumbled again when Milton told him he owed ten dollars for that rhyme.

"Class, we have a full day of learning ahead of us," Mrs. Baltman said. "I believe we have a math review, followed by a new science unit . . ."

Mrs. Baltman's phone began to ring.

"But first," the teacher said, "I believe I should answer my phone."

And that's just what Mrs. Baltman did.

Milton's teacher had a brief conversation with Ms. Kim. She was the first-grade teacher whose classroom was across the hall. Mostly, Mrs. Baltman said,  "Yes, Ms. Kim," "I see, Ms. Kim," and "Glad to, Ms. Kim" over and over again.

The call ended. Mrs. Baltman told the students that she needed two volunteers. All of them enthusiastically raised their hands.

7

"You are all so anxious to accept the mission," Mrs. Baltman said with surprise in her voice. "And yet, I haven't even told you what you'd be volunteering for."

All hands remained up.

"After all, it *could* be something sinister."

Some kids' hands went down.

"It *could also* be something dangerous."

More hands went down.

Only Milton, David, and Morgan were still volunteering when Mrs. Baltman announced that the special mission was . . .

What do you think the special mission is?

1 ☐ ☐ ☐ ☐ ☐ ☐ ☐ ☐ ☐ ☐

Meet Snowball

. . . **bringing Noah's extra** water dish to Ms. Kim's classroom. She needed it for Snowball, the class's new pet hamster.

AND AL
PLEASE T
AS A SP

"You are all so brave," Mrs. Baltman said. "Even though it's really only a job for one person, all three of you can go."

Milton, David, and Morgan stood up and attempted a triple high five. Milton missed and just swiped air. But that didn't really matter. The mission was theirs!

Milton led the way out of the classroom. Morgan carried the bottom of the water dish. David carried the top. The three second graders walked single file across the hall. Milton knocked on the door of Room 312C.

"Come in," Ms. Kim said.

The three students entered the room. They walked over to the hamster's cage. Morgan and David assembled the water dish. Milton said hello to Snowball.

"Thank you all so much for coming over so quickly," Ms. Kim said.

"Our pleasure, Ms. Kim," Milton said. "Fortunately, there was no traffic in the hallway."

Ms. Kim smiled. She kept smiling until . . .

Milton dimmed the lights and placed a flash drive into the classroom projector.

He then began a lecture on the care and feeding of a classroom pet.

"I call this lecture 'The Care and Feeding of a Classroom Pet,'" Milton said. "I have a lot of experience with Noah, our Room 311B ferret. And even though a ferret isn't a hamster, what I have to say will be very, very, very, very helpful."

"Very," Morgan added.

Milton cleared his throat and continued.

"Now, Snowball is your first classroom pet, so listen carefully. This shouldn't take more than three hours. Please write down everything I say. After I finish, there will be time for questions."

That's when Ms. Kim jumped in. She turned the lights back on and said, "Milton, it's very kind of you to offer us information—"

"Of course, Ms. Kim. But please turn the lights off again," Milton said.

"No, dear," Ms. Kim said. "Your lecture won't be necessary."

Ms. Kim gave Milton his flash drive. Then she put her arms around the three visiting students and walked them to the door.

"You see," Ms. Kim continued, "Snowball is the first classroom pet for *these* students. But I have had many other pets. I know all about taking care of an animal."

Milton shrugged and gave Snowball a gentle pat on the head. And with that, Morgan, David, and Milton left the classroom.

But first, Milton turned back and said, "I hope you do, Ms. Kim. I sure hope you do."

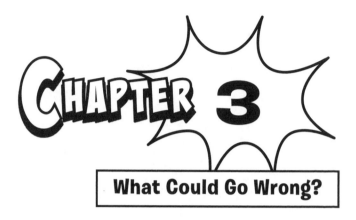

What Could Go Wrong?

The rest of the day went pretty much as usual in Room 311B. Well, Max Goen did lose his lucky pencil, which set off thirty minutes of chaos, but that's not really important. (He found it in his lunch bag right before a spelling quiz. *Whew!*)

Everything went fine in Room 312C as well. And after her first-grade class had gone home for the weekend, Ms. Kim stood alone at Snowball's cage.

"Have a wonderful Saturday and a beautiful Sunday, little Snowball," she said. "I've made sure that your water dish is full. And I'm leaving you plenty of delicious num-nums. Of course, I don't *know* that they're delicious. I've never tried them. But the package says they're good, so I am sure you'll like them. So long for now, precious . . ."

Ms. Kim paused for a moment, as if she were waiting for the hamster to say goodbye. But Snowball didn't utter a word, of course. Instead, she sort of shuddered.

"Oh, you poor dear," Ms. Kim said. "You must be shivering because you're cold! Well, don't you worry your pretty little furry head; I can fix that!"

Ms. Kim moved the grow light from a nearby plant so that it would warm Snowball. Of course, she first apologized to the plant. She told it that Snowball was chilly. The plant didn't respond.

Ms. Kim patted Snowball on the head and again said goodbye. Then the teacher left for the weekend.

All was quiet in Room 312C. Then Snowball began to feel the heat from the grow light. She instantly decided that it was too warm for her.

So she reached through the bars of her cage to try to turn off or move the light. But instead . . .

. . . she somehow switched the light to its brightest setting. At the same time, Snowball knocked over the homemade energy drink Ms. Kim had accidentally left behind. (It was a special bubbly blend that the teacher, a dedicated runner, made herself from fruits, grains, and other secret ingredients.)

The energy drink spurted into Snowball's water dish. Immediately, the hamster began lapping it up.

A hamster suddenly basking in a powerful grow light and filling up on a specially made energy drink—that's okay, right? Right? *RIGHT?*

Um, not exactly.

You've read three chapters! Amazing!

CHAPTER 4

The Hunger

By the next morning, the grow light had done something to Snowball. So had the energy drink.

Little Snowball was no longer little. In fact, since she'd burst right out of her cage, you might say she was giant-sized. Massive. Enormous. If that world records book had a category for biggest hamster, Snowball would've clearly earned the title.

As for energy . . . wow! The huge hamster had quickly eaten all her num-nums (too quickly to realize how delicious they actually were). Then she raced around the room. She ransacked the snack cupboard in search of more food. She wanted more. And more. And more.

Because it was Saturday, there weren't any student lunches in the classroom. And she'd already eaten all the snacks. So Snowball blasted out of Room 312C . . .

. . . and went in search of something (or some-*one*!) else to eat.

Snowball zipped in and out of all the open classroom doors. And if doors weren't open, she blasted right through them, creating a hamster-shaped doggy door where there hadn't been one.

She found a bag of pretzels on Principal Cooper's desk. They were stale, but Snowball ate them anyway.

She unearthed a few loose potato chips in the side pocket of the librarian's woolly sweater. (Don't ask.) She ate them too.

She spotted an apple on the poster outside the nurse's office.

She ate the apple. She even ate the word *apple*.

Snowball was one hungry hamster!

Then she moved on to the school cafeteria. She was sad to see that it was closed. She was sure there were many delectable treats on the shelves. But she simply had no way to get inside. (She tried to burst through the steel-reinforced doors, but they wouldn't budge.)

By the time Snowball got back to the Room 312C hallway, she'd covered every square inch of the school. She'd found all the food there was to be found.

But then . . . she heard a sound that brought instant joy to her enormous heart. It was the clear, unmistakable, happy sound of . . .

. . . chewing!

Snowball knew that the sound of chewing could mean only one thing:

FOOD!

And that food belonged to . . .

. . . none other than the one, the only . . .

CHAPTER 5

"Hoopy-neg, Hoopy-groo-ga!"

Noah!

Snowball bounded into Room 311B. She lumbered over to Noah's cage. She grabbed all his num-nums and gobbled them up in one gigantic gulp.

Stuck behind his extra-extra-extra-extra escape proof cage, Noah stared at Snowball in total disbelief. He was horrified.

Noah hadn't needed to use hamster-speak in

quite a while. But he thought back to his days at Critter Camp and came up with what he needed to say . . .

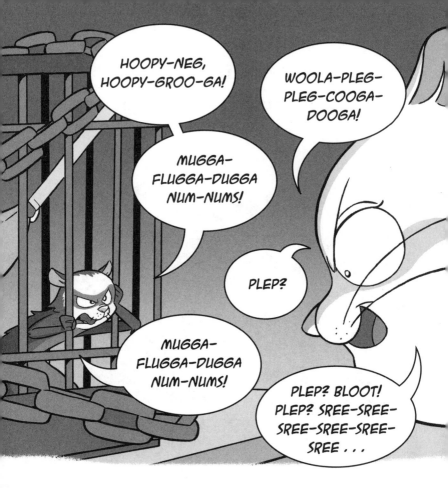

The chat went on for quite a while. Basically, Snowball told the ferret what had happened to make her so large. Noah said he was jealous. Then Noah told Snowball that no one was allowed to eat his num-nums. And Snowball was saying, "What num-nums? I don't see num-nums anymore!"

Snowball also told the ferret that she intended to take over the world. That really made Noah furious. After all, he assumed that the world was *his* to take over! *He* was the one who'd been planning world domination ever since he was just a little kit. (A *kit* is a baby ferret—in case you didn't know.)

HOOPY-GROO-GA!!!

Having to share his num-nums was bad enough. But Noah simply was *not willing* to share the whole world with a hamster, no matter how big she had become.

Snowball then said, "Na-na-na-na-na-na," which, incredibly, means the same thing in hamster and in English.

And with that, she was off. Off to take over the world.

Noah started panicking. So he leapt into action. Well, he leapt into as much action as a ferret can leap into while stuck in a cage. Noah paced. And while he paced, he thought things through.

He knew that Snowball had to be stopped. But he also knew that behind those bars, *he* couldn't stop her.

Noah was powerless. (He was also num-num-less, but he figured he'd deal with that later.) He realized that he needed someone to capture Snowball. And . . . it had to be someone who knew how to fight against evil classroom pets.

And then the hard-thinking ferret came up with the answer. He *knew* who could take on Snowball and win. And yet . . .

Noah wondered if it was too strange to reach out to the one person who'd always managed to stop *him* time after time. He wondered if it was ridiculous to ask for help from his arch-enemy. And he finally decided that Snowball absolutely had to be stopped. And that called for desperate measures. And so, he desperately called for . . .

CHAPTER 6

The Call

Mrs. Worthy!

The substitute teacher and superhero was driving her SUV, with her son, Milton, next to her in the passenger seat.

They were sitting in traffic, on their way to Milton's first meeting of the Happy Natures Club. Milton was dressed in the club's official gear. He was ready to study bugs, plants, and other wildlife. His fully packed backpack—including his lunch—was perched on his lap.

Milton and his mom were busy discussing the important differences between salami and bologna. Mrs. Worthy said that both were cured meats, and Milton wondered why lunchmeats needed to be cured. He asked how they got sick in the first place. Just as she was about to tell him that *cured* means cooking meats in a certain way . . .

. . . she was interrupted by a flashing and buzzing signal on the GPS screen! It was an urgent message for Mrs. Worthy. But it wasn't from Society of Substitutes headquarters . . . It was from Noah!

Fortunately, Mrs. Worthy was driving in the right-hand lane. She signaled and carefully pulled the SUV into a space in a supermarket parking lot.

Then the flashing and buzzing stopped, and

over the SUV's radio, Mrs. Worthy and Milton heard:

"Flegg! Chitter-blotch-chitter-num-nums-Snowball-gretch!"

"What is it, Mom?" Milton asked breathlessly.

"Flegg! Chitter-blotch-chitter-num-nums-Snowball-gretch!" Mrs. Worthy responded, forgetting that only she understood ferret-speak, thanks to her decoder wedding ring.

"I heard *that*, Mom," Milton said. "*But what does it mean?*"

Mrs. Worthy spoke clearly and calmly. But her words had a lot of panic in them.

"It means . . . 'Urgent! Snowball has turned into a giant hamster. She's on the loose at Beacher Elementary School! She took all the num-nums . . . and now she's ready to take over the world! Hurry! Your pal, Noah.'"

"I can't believe that, Mom," Milton exclaimed.

"You can't believe that Snowball is now a giant hamster and is looking to take over the world?" his mother asked.

"Well, yeah, that I believe," Milton said. "What I *can't* believe is that Noah called himself your pal."

"A ferret in need will say anything, son," Mrs. Worthy said.

Milton asked his mother if she thought Noah was telling the truth about Snowball. Mrs. Worthy agreed that it *could* be a devious plot by Noah, but she added there was no time to check.

"As a superhero, I live by the S.O.S. code of ethics, Milty. 'Save the world now, ask questions later,'" she said. She floored the SUV to drive to Beacher Elementary School.

On the way there, Mrs. Worthy had a speakerphone call with Chief Chiefman. He told her he would remotely unlock the side entrance to the gym so that she—and Milton—could enter the school. (Thanks to the exclusive Mega-Key 6233, made by the S.O.S. Gym Lock Division, he was able to do that!)

Mrs. Worthy's SUV screeched to a stop outside the gym door. The chief offered her an important final word:

"Stop Snowball . . . before this situation, um, snowballs!"

Friendly Enemies

Milton and his mom dashed out of the SUV and entered the school through the unlocked gym entrance. (Amazingly, Mrs. Worthy had been able to change into her S.O.S. outfit while driving *and* wearing a seat belt.) The pair made a beeline for Noah's cage in room 311B.

"Good. Noah is still safely locked inside his steel-reinforced cage," Mrs. Worthy noted with much relief in her voice. But she could see that the ferret was very upset. He babbled excitedly in ferret-speak. Each time he took a breath, Mrs. Worthy translated for Milton.

GREB-BLOTZ-MUCKY-MUCKY-SNOWBALL-DUNCH!

HE SAYS WE HAVE TO SAVE THE WORLD FROM SNOWBALL—SO HE CAN TAKE IT OVER SOMEDAY SOON.

LEELA-GRIBBLE-BLIBBLE-PIBBLE! BLEE-BLAH-NUM-NUMS!

HE DEMANDS THAT WE LET HIM JOIN US. BUT FIRST, HE DEMANDS MORE NUM-NUMS.

Mrs. Worthy returned to ferret-speak. She told Noah that she definitely wouldn't let him out of the cage. Then, in English, she told Milton to please refill Noah's num-nums from the travel bottle of num-nums in her purse. She'd learned the hard way to carry a bottle of num-nums at all times. She knew one day it would come in handy.

Milton emptied the travel bottle. Noah immediately ate up all the num-nums. The ferret wasn't really that hungry. He just wanted to finish them before Snowball returned.

Mrs. Worthy and Noah then had a private chat, all in ferret-speak. Noah told Mrs. Worthy everything he knew about how Snowball had become so ridiculously large. He told her he wished he had thought of growing that big. And he told her that Snowball was probably still in the school, hunting for more num-nums.

Mrs. Worthy informed Noah that it was weird to be on the same side for the first time ever. They were like friendly enemies. (Or as she'd heard such a thing was called—*frenemies*.) Noah snickered and told her not to get used to it. Once this matter was solved, he'd be ready for his next attempt at world domination. Mrs. Worthy snickered right back.

And with that, Mrs. Worthy waved goodbye to the ferret. She and Milton went off in search of Snowball. But before they left Room 311B, Noah offered an important final word:

"Vimka-voola-Snowball-degdeg!" (Which meant "Stop Snowball . . . before this situation, um, snowballs!")

What do you think happens next?

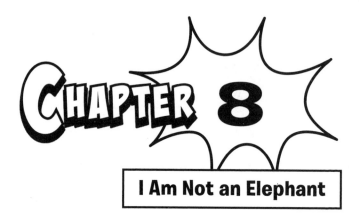

I Am Not an Elephant

"Here, Snowball. Here, little Snowball," Mrs. Worthy called as she and Milton ran up and down the halls in search of the ridiculously giant hamster.

No response.

"Maybe you want to try 'Here, Snowball. Here, *big* Snowball,'" Milton suggested.

Mrs. Worthy tried that.

No response.

"Let *me* try, Mom," Milton offered. "After

all, you're a stranger to Snowball. She knows me. I spent time with her yesterday, and as they always say, a hamster never forgets."

Mrs. Worthy corrected her son, telling him that people say that it's an *elephant* that never forgets. Milton said, "Oh yeah, I forgot. I guess I'm not an elephant." Then she told him he could certainly try calling Snowball, so he yelled, "Yo, Snowball . . ."

Still no response.

Mrs. Worthy put on her official S.O.S. fur-tracking eyeglasses. The glasses had built-in fur-sensing radar and came in seven fashionable styles. She and Milton started their search with the classrooms. They darted in and out of every single one. No Snowball. Next, they moved to the art room. No Snowball. Then the library and the gym—but Snowball wasn't in any of those places either.

The mother and son kept searching.

"She has to be here somewhere," Mrs. Worthy said. "After all, a gigantic hamster can't just disappear into thin air. Right, Milton? Am I right?"

Milton nodded. But truthfully, at that moment, he wasn't actually listening to what his mother was saying. Instead, he was busy going through his official Happy Natures backpack.

"There must be *something* in here that'll help us," Milton said.

He rummaged through the nature-themed items and pulled out . . . a pair of palm-sized, itty-bitty binoculars.

"Aha! Just perfect!" he yelled. He showed them to his mother. Then he put the binoculars up to his eyes.

"With these, I'll be able to find Snowball in no time!" he said.

Mrs. Worthy smiled. "Milty, dear, those mini-binoculars are very cute. But they're for looking at leaves and studying bugs or blades of grass. I don't think they'll work better than my official S.O.S. fur-tracking eyeglasses that see great distances and through walls . . ."

"Aha! What did I tell you? There. She. Is!" Milton exclaimed.

Mrs. Worthy couldn't believe it. But Milton wasn't kidding. Using the mini, not-that-powerful binoculars, he'd spotted Snowball scurrying into the music room. They followed her inside, slammed the door, and cornered the giant hamster right between two cellos!

Hangry Hamster

Snowball knew instantly she was trapped. But she wasn't too upset about that. Frankly, she was a little tired of running. Really she had been more *hangry* (that's being so hungry that you're angry) than interested in taking over the world.

"What now, Mom? What do we do now?" Milton wanted to know.

Snowball started jabbering. Unfortunately, Mrs. Worthy's decoder wedding ring didn't have a hamster-speak setting. So she didn't know that

Snowball was saying that the grow light helped her grow a little bit. But in truth, it was Ms. Kim's homemade bubbly energy drink that *really* filled her up.

Mrs. Worthy didn't understand a word. So she thought for a moment. And as she thought, well, the strangest thing happened.

Snowball let out a little gas.

(The fact is that a hamster can't burp—due to having a stomach that's split in two. So it's no secret where that gas came from. And while hamster farts are usually quiet and odorless, this was not a usual situation. The energy drink caused Snowball's gas to be both noisy and smelly.)

"Ugh! That has to be the all-time worst smell ever!" Milton yelled, holding his nose as his eyes began to water.

Mrs. Worthy agreed. She closed her eyes and held her nose at the same time.

Snowball let out another gust of wind. Then another.

The smell in the room was unbearable. And it was getting worse and worse with each hamster stink.

"Pee-you-a-dink-a-roo!" Milton yelled.

But it wasn't *all* bad news. Because when Milton and Mrs. Worthy finally took a breath and looked around, they noticed that . . .

. . . Snowball had gotten smaller!

"See, Mom! When Snowball releases gas, she shrinks!" Milton said.

"You're absolutely right, Milton," Mrs. Worthy said, in full agreement. "I wish Snowball could burp it all out. But being a hamster, she can't. So it's clear what we have to get Snowball to do."

Now, as a superhero, Mrs. Worthy had been in a lot of unusually challenging situations. But nothing came close to having to encourage a giant hamster (or anyone, for that matter) to pass gas.

"What are you going to do, Mom?" Milton asked.

"I have no idea," Mrs. Worthy admitted.

She knew that she should reach out to Chief Chiefman. But she also knew he'd probably laugh so hard that it would shake her transmitter helmet off her head.

Mrs. Worthy wanted to protect her son from the smelly smell, so she told him to leave the room. Normally, he would have argued and tried to stick around. But given how bad the room stunk, he followed her orders . . .

He watched through the window in the music room door as his mother tried to think of a way to get Snowball to pass gas.

First, Mrs. Worthy tried blowing a few notes on the tuba. She thought that maybe Snowball would want to copy the sound. Snowball didn't. Mrs. Worthy tried making noises with her armpits. No good. She got so desperate that she even thought about passing a little gas herself. Perhaps Snowball would take the hint.

But superheroes can't do that on command.

Mrs. Worthy was all out of fresh ideas. And almost out of fresh air. It was hard for her to think and hard for her to breathe. That's why it was good that in the hallway, Milton came up with a really, really, really good thought.

He left the music room door and quickly ran down the hall. In a flash, he came back carrying . . .

Only two chapters left to go! Great work!

1 2 3 4 5 6 7 8 9 ☐ ☐

Noah to the Rescue?

Noah!

Milton brought the ferret—still in his cage, of course—into the music room. Mrs. Worthy smiled at Milton for having done that. After all, she knew that Noah would do anything to stop Snowball. Surely he'd have a plan to get the hamster back to normal size.

In ferret-speak, Mrs. Worthy told Noah what was happening. She told him they needed Snowball to pass gas. Noah giggled. A lot. It was actually kind of cute, in a laughing-evil-ferret kind of way.

In ferret-speak, Noah told Mrs. Worthy that step one was to turn on the electric fan to help clear the air. She did that.

Then Noah leapt into action. From his cage, he spoke to Snowball in hamster-speak. Then he translated Snowball's response into ferret-speak so Mrs. Worthy could understand.

Noah informed Mrs. Worthy that Snowball understood what she had to do. But she could only release gas when she felt the need.

She couldn't do it on command. Noah then said he had an idea that would surely work. Mrs. Worthy told him to do his best. So . . .

. . . Noah looked into Snowball's eyes . . .

. . . and he blew her . . .

. . . a kiss!

Milton and his mother didn't know *why* it worked. They didn't know *how* it worked. But right after

Noah blew the kiss, they all heard . . .

Fzzzzzzzzzzzzzzzzzzzzzzzzzzzzzzzzzzzzzzzzzzz *zzzzzzzzzzzzzzzzzzzzzzzzzzzzzzzzrrfffff!!!*

The smell was unbelievable (though the fan did help).

And even more unbelievable was that when the sound stopped, Snowball had returned to her original adorable, cuddly size!

Milton had saved the day so Noah could save the day!

Milton picked up Noah's cage and walked him back to his classroom. It was good to be outside the music room, breathing the fresh, delightful hallway air.

The whole way back to Room 311B, Noah begged Milton to release him from the cage. He had helped save the world, after all. However, Milton didn't understand a word of ferret-speak, so Noah's urgent requests didn't matter.

Meanwhile, Mrs. Worthy gently carried Snowball back to Room 312C. She quickly placed her inside and reattached the cage's lid. She gave Snowball some clean water and a few num-nums (only a few!) for the weekend. And just to be sure, she moved the grow light far from Snowball's cage. Then she waved goodbye and rejoined Milton in the hallway between Room 312C and Room 311B.

With all back to normal (well, as normal as it ever gets at Beacher Elementary), Milton and his mom left the school. Mrs. Worthy made sure to lock the gym door. Then they went back to their SUV to get to the field to catch the end of the Happy Natures event.

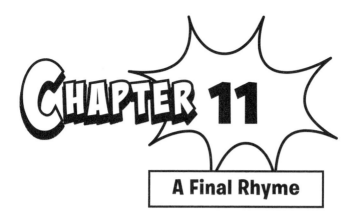

A Final Rhyme

The next night, Sunday, Milton was in his room, getting his backpack ready for the school week. And, thinking of Mrs. Baltman's awesome rhyming signs, he decided to make one of his own for the classroom. He created a sign that would rhymingly tell the whole school just what had happened . . .

Snowball the hamster got enormous
this weekend.

My mom the superhero and I jumped
in to prevent a bleak end.

Milton laughed, then decided that his verse wouldn't be worth ten dollars in the rhyme store. Besides, maybe it would be better if no one ever found out all that had gone on.

Meanwhile, at just that moment, inside Beacher Elementary School, Noah was busy making up his own rhyme. Based on one he had seen on the wall in 311B, it was all about his quest for world domination . . .

The hamster escaped, but now all is fine.
And soon the world will be mine. Mine. Mine. Mine. MINE!

The end. (For now.)

SUPER AWESOME GAMES

Think

In the story, Milton thinks Mrs. Baltman's rhymes are the best. Can you write a rhyming poem about something that happened to you recently?

Feel

In the story, Milton and his mom have to rush to the school to stop Snowball before it's too late. Was there ever a time that you had to rush to get somewhere important? Write about what happened and how you felt after.

Act

Milton and his mom have to help Snowball shrink back to her normal size. What's the biggest, scariest animal you've ever seen? Draw a picture of it.

Alan Katz has written more than forty books, including *Take Me Out of the Bathtub and Other Silly Dilly Songs*, *The Day the Mustache Took Over*, *OOPS!*, and *Really Stupid Stories for Really Smart Kids*. He has received many awards for his writing, and he loves visiting schools across the country.

Alex Lopez was born in Sabadell, a city in Spain near Barcelona. Alex has always loved to draw. His work has been featured in many books in many countries, but nowadays, he focuses mostly on illustrating books for young readers and teens.

READ THEM ALL!

And check out these other great **HarperChapters** series!